Ted's Tooth Trouble

Om KIDZ
An imprint of Om Books International

Om Kidz | Om Books International

Reprinted in 2023

Corporate & Editorial Office
A-12, Sector 64, Noida 201 301
Uttar Pradesh, India
Phone: +91 120 477 4100
Email: editorial@ombooks.com
Website: www.ombooksinternational.com

ISBN: 978-93-52760-35-0

Printed in India

10 9 8 7 6 5 4 3 2

Sales Office
107, Ansari Road, Darya Ganj
New Delhi 110 002, India
Phone: +91 11 4000 9000
Email: sales@ombooks.com
Website: www.ombooks.com

Ted's Tooth Trouble

Paste your photograph here

My name is

Ted is a **tiny** boy. He has been having a **terrible** day since **the time** he woke up.

Ted has **trouble talking** and **tasting. Tears trickle** down his cheeks.

He is very **upset** as he has a **terrible toothache.** Even a **tiny touch** pains **too** much. His **tooth** is about **to** fall.

Ted tries drinking warm water.

It helps with **toothache.**

All of a sudden, **the tooth** falls.

Ted runs to **tell** his mother. She **takes the tooth** from him and puts it **under** his pillow.

He doesn't **understand** why.
"What is **the use** of putting **the tooth under the** pillow?"
He asks her.

Ted's mother **tells** him **that** a **tooth** fairy will come **tonight.**

She will **take the tooth** from **under the** pillow.

The tooth fairy will leave a gift for **Ted.**

"Is it **true**?
Will **the tooth** fairy visit me?"
he **thinks.**

Ted has **trouble** falling asleep.

He gets inside his blanket.

He watches **the** door.

Soon **the** door handle **turns.**

The door opens.
A **tall** shadow walks
through the door.
Ted trembles with fear.

A shiver runs down from **the tip** of his hair to his **toes.**

Ted peeps out from
the top of **the** blanket.

To Ted’s surprise, the **tooth** fairy is not **tiny**. In fact, it looks like his Dad. **Ted** feels less scared.

He sees a big hand **take** away the **tooth** and leave a **tiny** gift on the **table**.

Ted sits up and sees the gift. He is not scared of **the tooth** fairy anymore.

Know your words

Naming words

Ted
tooth
umbrella
tears
toes

Describing words

tiny
true
terrible
tall

Doing words

talking
tells
trembles
tasting
take
understands
trickle
thinks
use
touch
turns

Sight words

trouble
thing
trick
toothache
tip
too
the
top
time
that
truth
through

Help the tooth fairy get to Ted's tooth.

Find the below words in the word search.

T	R	J	I	G	T	Y	H
T	U	C	N	A	F	I	C
O	T	I	Y	F	N	U	P
O	H	F	D	K	P	S	R
T	R	O	U	B	L	E	D
H	C	Q	N	G	D	K	K
Z	A	E	Q	N	E	M	E
B	W	Q	U	K	G	X	T

TROUBLE TOOTH

UNDER THING

TIP USE

Spot 5 differences between the given pictures.